Penworthy   1/02 $14.49   ETR

AUTHOR'S NOTE

Did King Arthur really exist? A book from 1136 called *A History of the Kings of Britain* says he did. It lists Arthur as a warrior king of the fifth century.

Whether or not he really lived, there are many wonderful songs, plays, and poems about Arthur. In some he is a good-hearted boy who became a great king. In others, he is a man who loved adventure more than he loved ruling.

In all of them, he is an example of what a king should be—kind, brave, and devoted to his people.

Written by Frank B. Edwards
Illustrated by John Bianchi
Copyright 1999 by Pokeweed Press

Cataloguing in Publication Data

Edwards, Frank B., 1952-
  Snug as a big red bug

(Pokeweed Press new reader series)

ISBN 1-894323-01-7 (bound)   ISBN 1-894323-00-9 (pbk.)

1. Insects—Juvenile fiction. I. Bianchi, John II. Title III. Series.

PS8559.D84S68 1999   jC813'.54   C99-900262-7
PZ7.E2535Sn 1999

Published by:
Pokeweed Press, Suite 200
17 Elk Court
Kingston, Ontario
K7M 7A4

Visit Pokeweed Press on the Net at:
www.Pokeweed.com

Send E-mail to Pokeweed Press at:
publisher@pokeweed.com

Printed in Canada by:
Friesens Corporation

American sales and marketing by:
Stoddart Kids
a division of Stoddart Publishing Co. Ltd.
180 Varick Street, 9th Floor
New York, New York 10014

Canadian sales and marketing by:
General Publishing
34 Lesmill Road
Toronto, ON
M3B 2T6

Visit General Publishing on the Net at:
www.genpub.com

Distributed in the U.S.A. by:
General Distribution Services
Suite 202
85 River Rock Drive
Buffalo, NY 14207

Distributed in Canada by:
General Distribution Services
325 Humber College Blvd.
Toronto, ON
M9W 7C3

Snug as a
Big Red Bug

Written by Frank B. Edwards
Illustrated by John Bianchi

Red Bug, Red Bug,
Where will you go?
Winter is coming,
With cold wind and snow.

I will live in this wool;
That's where I'll go.

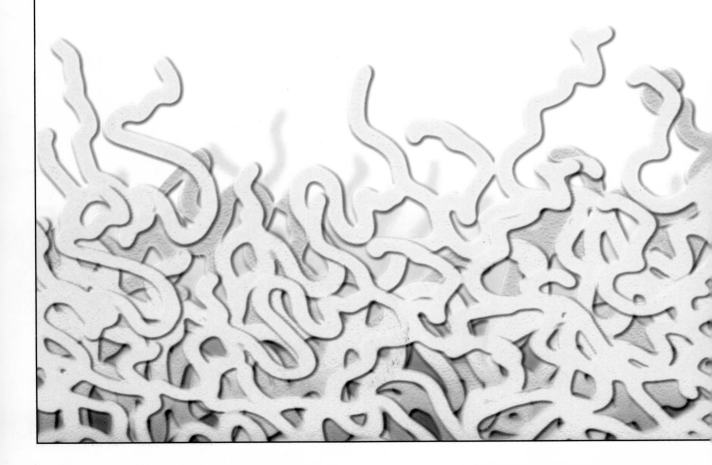

Oh, no you won't, Red Bug,
No way. Oh, no, no.

I will live in these feathers;
That's where I'll go.

Oh, no you won't, Red Bug,
No way. Oh, no, no.

I will live in this fur;
That's where I'll go.

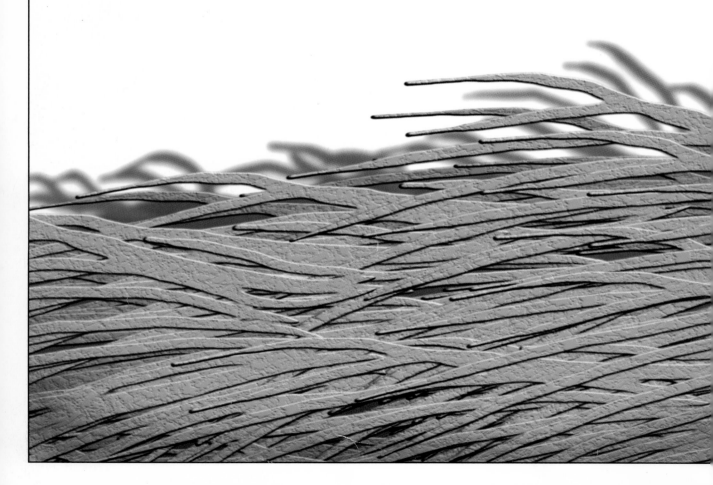

Oh, no you won't, Red Bug,
No way. Oh, no, no.

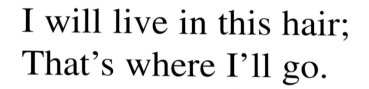

I will live in this hair;
That's where I'll go.

Red Bug, Red Bug,
Where will you sleep?
Winter is here,
And the snow is so deep.

I found this great place,
In Farmer Brown's rug.
I will stay here all winter,
As snug as a bug.

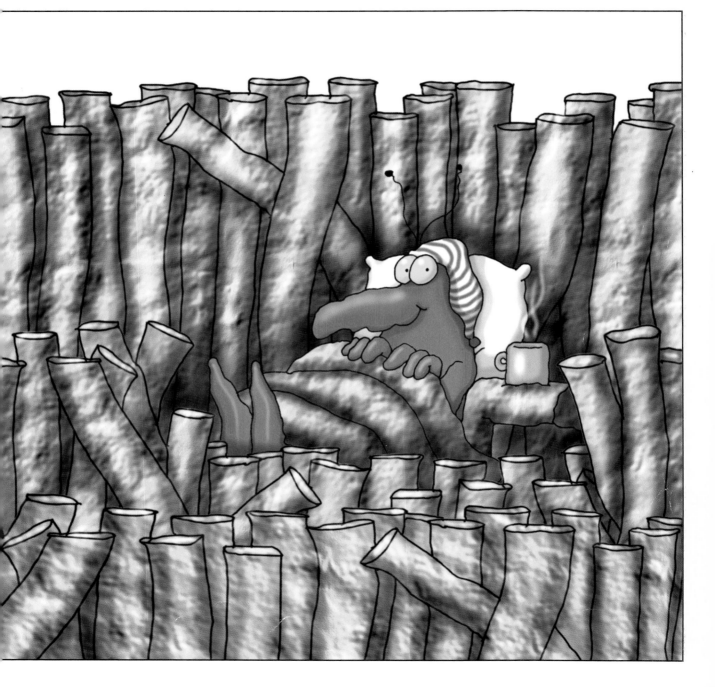

The End